ANNA SEWELL'S

BLACK BEAUTY

Retold for Little Children by

MARCIA MARTIN

Pictures by GEORGE SANTOS

Wonder® Books
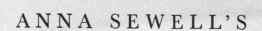 ALLAN PUBLISHERS, INC.
Exclusive Distributors

This book is a brief and simplified retelling of the famous story **BLACK BEAUTY**, that captures the spirit and beauty of the original tale. It is especially designed for very little folk. When the little folk are a little older, they will want to read the whole wonderful story, many times longer than this, just as it was written by Anna Sewell. Grosset & Dunlap, New York, publish the complete and unabridged text, with beautiful pictures in color and black and white.

1981 PRINTING

Published by GROSSET & DUNLAP, Inc.
Exclusively distributed by Allan Publishers, Inc.
Wonder® Books is a trademark of GROSSET & DUNLAP, INC.
ISBN: 0-8241-0595-8

DARKIE was a handsome horse. His shiny black coat was fine and soft. He had one white foot, and a pretty white star on his forehead. Darkie had lived on a big farm with many other horses ever since he was born. Now he was four years old, and about to be sold to Squire Gordon, who lived nearby.

As Squire Gordon rode Darkie home, he could tell that the black horse had been well trained. And Darkie could tell, by the squire's gentle hand on the reins, and the kind way he talked to him, that his new master would treat him well. When they reached home, the squire's wife and two little girls, Jessie and Flora, were waiting for them.

"Oh, what a beautiful horse!" they cried.

"Yes," agreed Squire Gordon. "His name is Darkie. But he is such a handsome horse, I think he should have another name. Don't you?"

"How about Black Beauty?" asked Mrs. Gordon.

"Black Beauty," said the squire slowly. "Yes, that is a very good name for him."

Black Beauty was happy at Squire Gordon's. There were several other horses, but he soon became the favorite. Not only did the squire like him best, but the two little girls loved the gentle horse. They often came to pet him and to take rides on him.

Late one night, Squire Gordon hurried into
the stable.

"I am sorry to disturb you at this hour, Joe,"
the squire said to Joe Green, the boy who took
care of the horse. "But Mrs. Gordon is very ill,
and I must ride for the doctor."

Quickly Joe saddled Black Beauty and Squire Gordon galloped away. Black Beauty knew that something was wrong and that his master was in a great hurry. The horse ran as fast as he could.

When Squire Gordon reached the doctor's house, it was three in the morning. He rapped loudly at the door.

"Will you please come at once?" Squire Gordon begged the doctor. "My wife is very ill."

"Of course I will come," replied the doctor. "But my horse has gone lame. May I ride yours?"

"Black Beauty is very tired," the squire said. "We galloped all the way over. But I am sure he will get you there. Take him and I will walk."

The doctor dressed quickly, climbed up on Black Beauty, and away they went. The doctor was much heavier than Squire Gordon and not nearly so good a rider. But Black Beauty, even though he was almost exhausted, ran as fast as he could. It was beginning to grow light when they arrived home, and the doctor went to the house.

Little Joe Green led Black Beauty back to the stable. The horse's body was soaking wet, and he could hardly stand. Joe rubbed Beauty's legs and chest, and gave him some water to drink. But Joe did not know that he should have covered him with warm blankets, and given him hot food instead of water. Joe loved horses, but this was his first job, and he had much to learn.

Soon Black Beauty began to shake and tremble, and he felt terribly cold. He lay in his stall, shivering, for what seemed like a long, long time.

Finally, Squire Gordon arrived home. He was very tired after his long walk, but he saw immediately what had happened. He covered Black Beauty with warm blankets, gave him a little hot water to drink, and called the horse doctor.

Black Beauty was very sick. Poor Joe Green came every day to see him, and to tell him how sorry he was. Squire Gordon and the horse doctor nursed Beauty and at last he began to get better.

One day, when Black Beauty was well again, Squire Gordon and Joe came to see him.

"I will certainly be sorry to lose this horse," Squire Gordon said to Joe. "You know he saved

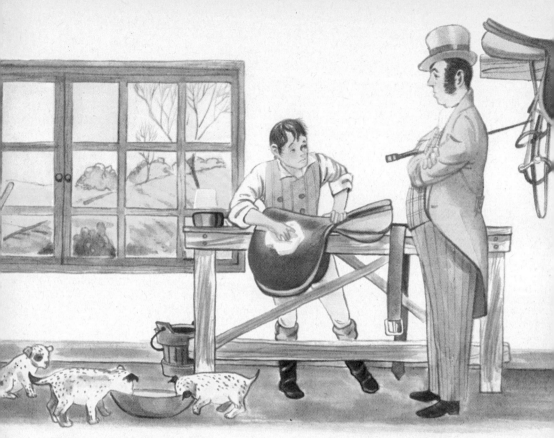

Mrs. Gordon's life when she was so ill. Now she is better, but the doctor says we must move to a warmer place."

"What will happen to your house?" asked Joe.

"We shall close it," the squire answered. "And we shall have to sell the horses. A friend of mine needs a stableboy, Joe. Will you work for him?"

Joe nodded, and walked out of the stable sadly with his master.

Not long after this, the squire, Mrs. Gordon and the two little girls came down to the field to say good-by.

"We will never forget you, Black Beauty," whispered the squire's wife. The horse lowered his head, and the two children patted him gently for the last time.

After he left the Gordons, Black Beauty had
many masters. Finally he was bought by a man
who used him to pull a cab. The cab carried people,
and their heavy bags and trunks, from the railroad
station to their homes. Beauty was outside in all
kinds of weather. Even when it was freezing cold
or snowing hard, he had to pull the cab over the
slippery streets. And though he was often tired and
hungry, he always did his best.

But finally he became too weak to work at all,
and his master took him to a horse sale to be sold.

Many people looked at Black Beauty, but no
one wanted to buy a horse that looked so old and
tired and thin. At last a tall man with a mustache
saw him.

The man looked at him carefully. "I once
knew a horse that looked like him. What is his
name?" the man asked.

"Black Beauty is his name," answered the owner. "And I will sell him cheap, because he is too old to work any longer."

"I knew he must be Black Beauty!" the man exclaimed joyfully. "Oh, Beauty, don't you remem-

ber me? I'm Joe Green, the stableboy who made you so ill many years ago."

Beauty didn't recognize him, because Joe was a grown man now. But the horse was very glad to find a friend. Joe bought him from the cab driver and led Beauty to his new home.

When they reached the house, two women came down the steps and looked at the black horse.

"Why it's Black Beauty!" they cried, as they flung their arms about the horse's neck.

"Do you remember us, Beauty?" asked Miss Flora. "You're back at Squire Gordon's. And we're the same little girls, grown up now, who used to take rides on you many years ago."

"I've never forgotten you, Beauty," said Joe. "And you taught me a lesson I've never forgotten, either."

"None of us ever forgot you, Beauty," agreed Miss Jessie. "And we'll never, never sell you again."

Black Beauty was with his old friends once more, and would never have to leave again the fields he loved so much.